MR. COOL

Roger Hargreaves

Written and illustrated by
Adam Hargreaves

Poor Jack Robinson wasn't feeling very well.

He had been in bed for days and he had to stay in bed until he was better.

"I'm bored," he huffed. "I wish I could go outside and play with my friends."

Suddenly, a blue blur shot in through the open window.

It looped-the-loop around the light in the ceiling and a small blue figure, wearing a hat, landed on the end of Jack's bed.

"Cool!" said Jack.

"That's me. Mr Cool," said Mr Cool.

"Cool!" repeated Jack.

"You look a bit bored," said Mr Cool. "I thought we could go and have some fun."

"I wish I could," said Jack, "but I'm not allowed out of bed."

"I think we could make an exception just this once," said Mr Cool, and he clicked his fingers.

The next instant Jack found himself sitting in the cockpit of a jet aeroplane.

"Why don't you take it out for a spin?" suggested Mr Cool.

"What? Can I really fly it?" said Jack.

"Sure you can," said Mr Cool. "It's easy!"

So Jack flew the jet-plane out across the Atlantic Ocean and back.

"That was cool," cried Jack, when they were back on the ground. "Thanks, Mr Cool!"

"We haven't finished yet," said Mr Cool and he clicked his fingers again.

Jack heard a crowd roar. He was at a football ground, but he wasn't sitting in the crowd. He was on the bench with the other players!

And he was even wearing the team strip!

"Quick!" said Mr Cool. "The manager wants you to go on."

"He wants me to play?" said Jack, incredulously. "But they're Capital United!"

And you'll never guess what . . .
Jack scored the winning goal!

"Wow! That was so cool!" said Jack.

As Jack walked off the pitch Mr Cool clicked his
fingers and whisked them away.

To climb the tallest tree in the world!

He clicked his fingers again and before you could say Jack Robinson . . .

. . . they were standing on top of a mountain!

"Where are we?" called Jack, over the noise of the wind.

"Mount Everest!" said Mr Cool.

"How cool! What are we doing here?" shouted Jack.

"Sledging!" said Mr Cool. "Let's go!"

Jack and Mr Cool slid from the very top to the very bottom of Mount Everest.

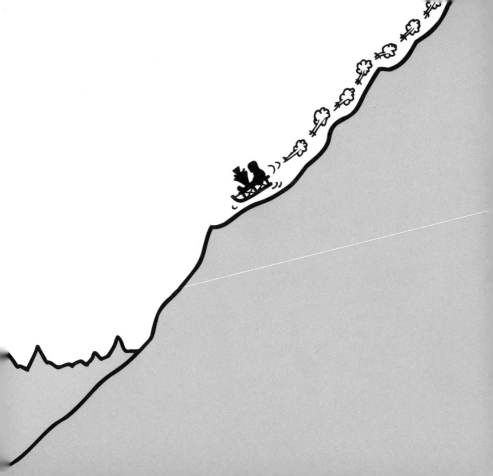

"That was the coolest thing ever!" cried Jack.

"It was more like the c . . . c . . . coldest," stuttered Mr Cool.

For the final time that day Mr Cool clicked his fingers.

In an instant Jack found himself back in his bedroom.

"Thank you so much, Mr Cool," said Jack.
"That was . . ."

". . . amazing?!" laughed Mr Cool.

"Well, I'll be off," said Mr Cool. "But there's one more thing, Jack. Have a look in the mirror."

With this, Mr Cool shot out through the open window.

Jack went into the bathroom and looked in the mirror.

"Cool!" said Jack when he saw himself.

And why do you think Jack was so pleased?

That's right, all his spots had gone. Jack was better.

I wonder, on which page did Jack get better?

Fantastic offers for Mr. Men fans!

Collect all your Mr. Men or Little Miss books in these superb durable collectors' cases!
Only £5.99 inc. postage and packing, these wipe-clean, hard-wearing cases will give all your Mr. Men or Little Miss books a beautiful new home!

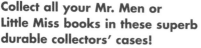

Keep track of your collection with this giant-sized double-sided Mr. Men and Little Miss Collectors' poster.
Collect 6 tokens and we will send you a brilliant giant-sized double-sided collectors' poster! Simply tape a £1 coin to cover postage and packaging in the space provided and fill out the form overleaf.

STICK £1 COIN HERE
(for poster only)

Only need a few Mr. Men or Little Miss to complete your set? You can order any of the titles on the back of the books from our Mr. Men order line on 0870 787 1724. Orders should be delivered between 5 and 7 working days.

— TO BE COMPLETED BY AN ADULT —

To apply for any of these great offers, ask an adult to complete the details below and send this whole page with the appropriate payment and tokens, to: MR. MEN CLASSIC OFFER, PO BOX 715, HORSHAM RH12 5WG

☐ Please send me a giant-sized double-sided collectors' poster.

AND ☐ I enclose 6 tokens and have taped a £1 coin to the other side of this page.

☐ Please send me ☐ Mr. Men Library case(s) and/or ☐ Little Miss library case(s) at £5.99 each inc P&P

☐ I enclose a cheque/postal order payable to Egmont UK Limited for £..

OR ☐ Please debit my MasterCard / Visa / Maestro / Delta account (delete as appropriate) for £..

Card no. ☐☐☐☐ ☐☐☐☐ ☐☐☐☐ ☐☐☐☐ ☐☐☐☐ ☐☐☐☐   Security code ☐☐☐

Issue no. (if available) ☐   Start Date ☐☐/☐☐/☐☐   Expiry Date ☐☐/☐☐/☐☐

Fan's name: ....   Date of birth: ....

Address: ....

....

Postcode: ....

Name of parent / guardian: ....

Email for parent / guardian: ....

Signature of parent / guardian: ....

Please allow 28 days for delivery. Offer is only available while stocks last. We reserve the right to change the terms of this offer at any time and we offer a 14 day money back guarantee. This does not affect your statutory rights. Offers apply to UK only.

☐ We may occasionally wish to send you information about other Egmont children's books. If you would rather we didn't, please tick this box.   **Ref: MRM 001**